GUS and GRANDPA
and the Halloween Costume

Claudia Mills ★ Pictures by Catherine Stock

Farrar, Straus and Giroux

New York

For Ian James Seabrooke
— C.M.

For Rell
— C.S.

Text copyright © 2002 by Claudia Mills
Illustrations copyright © 2002 by Catherine Stock
All rights reserved
Distributed in Canada by Douglas & McIntyre Ltd.
Color separations by Phoenix Color Corporation
Printed and bound in the United States of America by Phoenix Color Corporation
First edition, 2002
1 3 5 7 9 10 8 6 4 2

Library of Congress Cataloging-in-Publication Data
Mills, Claudia.
    Gus and Grandpa and the Halloween costume / Claudia Mills ;
pictures by Catherine Stock.— 1st ed.
        p. cm.
    Summary: Second-grader Gus wants a store-bought Halloween
costume to wear to school, but because he knows his parents do
not believe in buying costumes, he turns to his grandfather for help.
    ISBN 0-374-32816-1
    [1. Halloween—Fiction. 2. Grandfathers—Fiction.] I. Stock,
Catherine, ill. II. Title.

PZ7.M63963 Gudi 2002
[E]—dc21

                                                        2001023151

Contents

No Costume

It was almost Halloween,
and Gus still didn't
have a costume.
In kindergarten
he had been a cowboy.
In first grade
he had been a pirate.
What could he be this year?

"Let's use our imaginations,"
  Gus's mother said.
  Gus knew this meant
  that she didn't want
  to buy anything.
  Gus's mother didn't believe
  in store-bought costumes.

Gus's father also didn't believe
in store-bought costumes.
"All this fuss about Halloween!"
he said.
"When I was a kid
we wore any old thing
we could find
lying around the house."

Gus looked around the house.
Maybe he could be a ghost.
He tried putting an old sheet
over his head.
But he had never heard of
any ghosts who wore
pink-flowered sheets.

Maybe Gus could be a mummy.
He tried wrapping the sheet
tightly around him.
But he had never heard of
any pink-flowered mummies,
either.

"What are you going
to be for Halloween?"
Ryan Mason asked Gus
in school the next day.

"I don't know," Gus said.
"What about you?"

"I'm not telling," Ryan said.

"But here is a clue.

The cape is black.

The fangs look like real fangs.

The blood looks like real blood."

Gus could guess:

Ryan was going to be a vampire.

Gus wished he could be

a vampire, too.

But Gus knew
he wouldn't find
a cape or fangs or blood
lying around his house.
And he knew his mother
wouldn't buy him any.
She thought gory
store-bought costumes
were the worst of all.

Gus's only hope
was Grandpa's house.
Maybe he could find
a costume there.

Picking Pumpkins

On Sunday,
Gus's father took him
to Grandpa's house.
"How are your pumpkins doing?"
Daddy asked.

Gus ran outside to check.
He and Grandpa had planted
pumpkin seeds last spring.
Now there were five plump
pumpkins on the vines,
ready to be picked.

Gus counted them again.
Five pumpkins,
big and round and gold,
lying in Grandpa's cornfield
like a pirate's treasure.

Maybe Gus should be
a pirate again.
But he knew Ryan
would never be the same thing
two times in a row.

Grandpa cut four of the pumpkins
from their stems
with his sharp pocketknife.
"Here, Gus,
you can cut the last one,"
Grandpa said.
He helped Gus cut
the biggest pumpkin of all.

Then Gus and Grandpa
loaded the pumpkins
into the wheelbarrow.
Gus wheeled it carefully
to the house,
with Skipper barking all the way.

Maybe Skipper could be part
of Gus's Halloween costume.
Gus could be a dogcatcher,
and Skipper could be the dog
he was trying to catch.
Having a dog
as part of your costume
would be almost as cool
as real-looking fangs
and real-looking blood.

Then Gus remembered:
dogs weren't allowed at school.
Gus felt like giving up.

The Costume

"Do you have any Halloween
costumes in your shed?"
Gus asked Grandpa
as they sat with Daddy
at the kitchen table,
admiring their pumpkins.

23

Gus had learned
that almost anything
could be found
in Grandpa's broken-down,
falling-down,
tumbling-over
back shed—
except for shiny new
fangs and blood.
Still, a musty, dusty costume
would be better than
no costume at all.

Gus's father turned to him.
"Can't you just use an old sheet
and be a ghost or a mummy?"

Gus didn't reply.
His dad didn't understand.

"Come on," Grandpa said to Gus.
"There's nothing in the shed,
  but I might have something
  here in the house."

In a bedroom
where no one slept,
Grandpa dug in the closet
and found a chest.
It was a dusty, musty chest.
Gus knew it would be.

"Look in there,"
  Grandpa told Gus.

Inside the chest,
Gus found pretty aprons
and fancy handkerchiefs
and a lady's beaded purse.

"Whose are these?" Gus asked.
They didn't look like
Halloween costumes.

"They belonged
to your grandma,"
Grandpa said.
Grandma had died
before Gus was born.
"Keep looking."

Then, at the bottom of the chest,
Gus found something else:
a small bright-red jacket
with shiny gold buttons
and a black belt,
and a broad-brimmed hat.

"Try them on," Grandpa said.

Gus did.
They fit!

"It's a Canadian Mountie
costume," Grandpa said.
"The Mounties are famous
policemen in Canada
who ride on horses.
Would you like to be
a Canadian Mountie
for Halloween?"

"Sure!" Gus said.
He ran to look at himself
in Grandpa's mirror.
He looked super-cool.
But would Ryan think
it was okay to wear a
hand-me-down costume?

Gus's father came in
and saw Gus.
"That looks familiar," Daddy said.

"It should," Grandpa told him.
"That was your Halloween
costume one year.

You had your heart set
on being a Canadian Mountie,
and you wouldn't hear
of anything else.
What a fuss you made!
Your mama finally had
to figure out how to sew
this for you."

Gus giggled.

"I have a picture of your daddy
in this costume," Grandpa said.
"Let's see if I can find it."

Grandpa took a big photo album
from the shelf.

The pictures in it
were black-and-white.
In the pictures,
Grandpa was young.
Grandma was smiling.
Daddy was a little boy.
Aunt Sue was a baby.

"Here it is."
Grandpa pointed.

There was Gus's father,
wearing the Canadian Mountie
costume and smiling.
"Hmm," Daddy said.
"Yup, that's me all right."

Gus stared.
The people all looked so different,
but the costume looked
just the same.
Gus loved his costume
more than ever.

Grandpa patted his arm.
Then they put the pictures away.

Halloween

On Halloween,
Gus had the best costume
in the whole second grade,
even better than Ryan Mason's.
Ryan's fangs and blood
looked real and scary.

But four other kids had
the very same costume,
fangs and blood and cape and all.

"Where did you buy
your costume?"
Ryan asked Gus.

"I didn't buy it," Gus said.
"My grandma made it for Daddy
when he was a little boy."

Gus waited to hear
what Ryan would say.

"Wow," Ryan said.

"That is so cool."

After school,
Grandpa came to Gus's house
with three pumpkins.
They carved jack-o'-lanterns
and put candles inside.

45

Right before trick-or-treating,
Gus's dad snapped a picture
of Gus in his costume.
"Like father, like son," he said.

Gus gave his biggest smile.
He wanted to look
exactly like Daddy
in the picture.

But his picture
would be even better than
Daddy's—
it would have Grandpa in it.